The Battle of Mohegan Bluffs
Block Island Settlement Series — Book I

History Brought to Life

David Lee Tucker

1

Introduction

The Mohegan Bluffs of Block Island were named after a band of Mohegan Indians who came to Block Island, and were destroyed by the local Manissean Indians at the Island's tallest bluffs, located on the Southeast corner of the Island.

I have heard many versions of this story over the years. But, even after hearing it for the first time when I was ten years old, I wondered about how it all happened. Why did the two tribes fight in the first place? What did it look like? Why did they come to fight at that location? Did the Manisseans literally push or throw the Mohegans off the bluffs?

In this book, I have taken what little documented information I could find and pieced together *a fictional account* of how this action might have taken place. Based on this little information it appears that a small Mohegan war party landed on Block Island at a west side beach and, somehow, they were driven by the Island's Manissean Indians southeast to the tallest bluffs on the Island. This band of Mohegans was either driven off the bluffs and/or were trapped there until they starved to death.

In S.T. Livermore's, *History of Block Island,* he records the account of Reverend Samuel Niles describing the action on pages 56 & 57 with the following:

"The Indians on this Island had war with the Mohegan Indians, although the Island lies in the ocean and open seas, four leagues from the nearest mainland, and much farther distant from any Island, and from the nearest place of landing to the Mohegan country forty miles, I suppose at least, through a hideous wilderness, as it then was, besides the difficulty of two large rivers. To prosecute their designed hostilities each party furnished themselves with a large fleet of canoes, furnished with bows and arrows.

"It happened at the same time the Mohegans were coming here in their fleet to invade the Block Islanders, they were going with their fleet to make spoil on the Mohegans. Both being on the seas, it being in the night arid moonshine, and by the advantage of it the Block Islanders discovered the Mohegans, but they saw not the Islanders. Upon which these turned back to their own shore, and hauled their canoes out of sight, and waylaid their enemies until they landed, and marched up in the Island, and then stove all their [the Mohegans'] canoes, and drove them to the opposite part of the Island, where, I suppose, the cliffs next the sea are near, if not more than two hundred feet high, and in a manner perpendicular, or rather near the top hanging over, and at the bottom near the seashore very full of rocks. [Near the new light—house.] They could escape no farther. Here these poor creatures were confined, having nothing over them but the heavens to shelter or cover them, no food to support them, no water to quench their thirst. Thus, they were kept destitute of every comfort of life, until they all pined away and perished in a most miserable manner, without any compassion in the least degree shown to them. They had indeed by some means dug a trench around them toward the land to defend them from the arrows of their enemies, which I have seen, and it is called the Mohegan Fort to this day."

That fort, probably, has long since sloughed off into the sea by the action of frosts and rains upon the bluffs for more than a century. All personal knowledge of it has also faded away from the Islanders.

In my 'research' I could find no definitive date as to when the battle occurred. However, Livermore's *History of Block Island* provides some clues. He references Reverend Niles, writing on page 50 that, "Mr. Niles, born upon Block Island, in 1674, in his youth conversed freely with the old natives, as well as read and conversed with the best informed on the mainland concerning the Indians. He, in the main, is good authority." He also recorded Niles stating on page 56 — "They were perpetually engaged in wars one with another, long before the English settled on Block Island, and perhaps before any English settlements were made in this land, according to the Indians' relation, as some of the old men among them informed me when I was young." So, Reverend Niles was acquainted with the old Indians who may have had firsthand knowledge of the battle when they were younger.

On page 69 Livermore writes of Block Island "Still, it was within reach of the eagle—eyed Sassacus and his warlike Pequots, and even the more distant Mohegans beyond the Connecticut river coveted the fertile plantations and productive fishing grounds of Manisses."

Sassacus was a powerful Pequot Sachem who did not become the grand sachem of the Pequots until 1632 after the grand sachem Tatobem was killed in that year. And he mentions, "The Mohegan Bluffs will ever remain as a monument of the Narragansett's' victory over the Mohegans, and the friendship of Ninicraft their chief with the English will also immortalize his strategy in maintaining his grounds against the more warlike Pequots."

Livermore and Niles seem to put Ninicraft and Sassacus, sachems of the early 1600's, as being around at the time of the Battle of Mohegan Bluffs.

In addition, for several centuries the Mohegans were part of the Pequot tribe but in 1632 due to the death of grand sachem Tatobem creating internal divisions, Sachem Uncas and his followers separated from the Pequot main body to become more uniquely identified as Mohegans. The battle may have happened after this occurred for the invaders to have been clearly identified as Mohegan and not as Pequot.

Livermore also comments on page 69 stating the following: "Of conflicts here between the Indians our knowledge is only traditionary. This knowledge, however, is sufficient to leave the conviction that from "time out of mind," this Island was a bone of contention between neighboring tribes upon the main—land. As it lies nearest to the territory occupied by the Narragansetts it naturally came under the rule of their Chiefs, Ninicraft, Miantinomo, Canonicus, and other more remote sachems in past ages." All of the Indian chiefs mentioned were living in the first half of 1600.

In William P. Sheffield's *A Historical Sketch of Block island,* he too mentions that Rev. Samuel Niles in his, *History of the French and Indian Wars,* saying that "long before the English settled the Island, and perhaps before there was any white settlement in this land, as he was told by some of the old men among the Indians, when the Mohegans and the Narragansets were at war," Sheffield repeats that the story was told by the "old men" suggesting they had firsthand knowledge. If it was a story passed down by oral tradition then any of the Manissean tribe could have shared it with Niles.

While none of this "evidence" provides a conclusive time for the Manissean victory at Mohegan Bluffs, it provides me with indications that the battle may have occurred more closely to the early European settlement in the 1600's than had been previously thought.

"He has redeemed my soul in peace from the battle" - Psalm 55:18

The story incorporates the following historical figures and fictional characters:

Manisseans
- Jacquantu – Historical Manissean Sachem (Chief)
- Penewess – Historical Manissean Minor Sachem
- Audsah – Historical Manissean Indian Brave thought to have ties to the Pequot Tribe. (Involved in the murder of Captain John Oldham setting off the Pequot War)
- Asesakes – Fictitious young Manissean Indian Brave
- Alsoomse – Fictitious young Manissean Indian Girl

Mohegans
- Quttajuia – Fictitious Mohegan lower sachem who led the attack on the Manisseans and was driven to the Mohegan bluffs.
- Mingan, (Gray wolf) – Fictitious older Mohegan Brave
- Kitchi – Fictitious Younger Mohegan Brave. Cousin of Quttajuia

A map incorporating the story locations and tracking the Mohegans flight is provided at the end of the story in Appendix I

Authentic Algonquin words are included in the dialogue of the story. Their meaning can be gleaned from the context but a dictionary is provided at the end of the book in Appendix IV

Chapter 1

September 1633
Manisses (Block Island)

A fiery sun kissed the western horizon setting it ablaze. The young Manissean Indian gasped seeing the sweat from his own bronze skin appear set on fire. He pressed on driving his legs up the steep hundred—foot slope, churning sand and gravel in his wake. His insides burned with each heave of his chest. *Others are waiting, I cannot stop.* He took a peak over at the eastern sky, the moon was already visible.

Even with his leathery feet, calloused from the rocky soil of Manisses Island, each footfall drove the sharp gravel into his soles, knifing the pain up into his legs. In between groans he challenged himself choking out loud, "I am not a cub, I am a brave!"

The boy drove on. He wondered, *Why me? Fastest runner I am not.* Still, he knew why. *Am I cursed to have eyes of an eagle?*

Jacquantu, the tribe's elder sachem, had ordered Asesakes— *"One Who Sees What Other's Cannot"*—to do this important task. The boy's chest swelled with pride but now he called down to the war party, "Do not leave without me!"

Before the Manissean braves paddled off to surprise the Mohegans on the long island, Asesakes was charged with taking one final look toward Montauk to make sure that no Mohegan war party was paddling toward Manisses. They did not want to leave the rest of the tribe in danger. But, Asesakes had heard the grumbling from the older braves as he ran toward the high ground. They also did not want to wait.

Jacquantu was a cunning leader with much *wáwôtam*, but many of the braves, including Penewess the lower sachem from west of the great pond, often said the older leader was too careful.

The Manissean tribe had never sought battle with the mainland tribes, but the last time the warriors from Montauk had come forty of the island people were killed. Much of their clam, scallop, oyster, and mussel beds were pillaged. Penewess's blood was hot. He had convinced many of the others that it was time for war. Reluctantly, Jacquantu had bowed to the passion of Penewess and the younger men.

Asesakes glanced down to the beach at the one hundred men standing alongside a dozen dugout canoes filled with bows, arrows, clubs, stone axes, and hatchets. They were waiting for him and would be angry if they had to wait very long. *I must hurry!*

Earlier Asesakes had joined the older braves as Penewess led them to catch seals and split them open. The

9

young brave followed the others scooping out the warm, bloody fat—eating and choking it down. He too painted his face with the gore and chanted war songs. They all danced to the sound of tomahawks pounding on driftwood logs. *Am I now fully an 'Inak' brave?* he wondered.

Just a few more strides. His chest burned. He reached the narrow top plateau and stumbled over the sparse tufts of tall grass, falling to his knees. Asesakes gulped in the cool salty air and gathered his strength to stand. *I cannot delay the warriors and draw their mucuhcôqak kisqutu.* But, even more than the angry spirits of his clansmen he feared losing his place in the war canoes.

He looked west. Only half of the sun disk was still visible. The young brave shaded his eyes. Asesakes could barely make out the shadow of the long island on the horizon. "*Mikucut!*" he cursed; even now, the glare from the setting sun blinded his vision. He would have to wait until the sun had dipped completely below the horizon.

The boy paced back and forth pounding his fists together while staring at the sinking sun. He begged it to move faster, crying out, "*Kipi!*"

At last the final, glowing arc blinked, dipping below the rim of the world. He looked out to sea to scan the shimmering surface of the darkening waves for any threat, anything that looked amiss.

Nothing. Good. My job is done and I can return.

He bit his lip. The news was good but, would the older braves beat him for wasting their time? Asesakes turned toward the west beach and waved his arms, repeatedly crossing them to signal that all was clear.

The war party did not hesitate and began launching their canoes into the surf. Asesakes' eyes widened as his jaw dropped. They were leaving him behind! *No!*

"*Mutu! Mutu!*" he shouted, trying to get the attention of someone—anyone. Penewess must have convinced Jacquantu that they should not wait any longer.

I must go, now! Asesakes turned and took several strides, jumping off the edge of the high, gravel hill to race down to the boats.

What? He jammed his heels into the loose, sharp gravel and the pain shot from his feet, up to his body and into his brain. "*Aghhh!*" he screamed but forced himself to focus on a distant motion.

He peered to the northwest. *Was there something out in the water? Yes, little flashes of light. A churning school of fish or whales?* He squinted and stilled his breath, concentrating on the barely visible motion. *Paddles dipping in and out of the water, numerous and steady.* His eyes widened. *Mohegans!* A raiding party was coming, not from Montauk, but from Quinnehtukqut.

A knot twisted in the boy's stomach. If the Manissean warriors left now, the island would be defenseless. Asesakes spun back toward the beach and cupped his hands around his mouth. He yelled to stop them. "*Ahqi! Ahqi!*" The canoes kept moving away. He screamed out a wôpsukuhq eagle cry, but it did not stop the canoes.

Hurling himself down the slope Asesakes bolted for the beach, screaming out "*Ahqi!*" Racing down the narrow path through dense brush and trees, he stumbled over thick, round roots and tripped over rocks. Reaching the shore dunes, he plowed through the deep sand and tall reeds.

Some young children, along with the women lingered on the beach, watching the men paddle away. They turned to stare at him. Asesakes staggered toward the surf. The last canoe was not too far away, but it was moving fast. He grabbed the back of his leg. His muscles were cramping. *I will never be able to catch them by swimming.*

What can I do? There were no more canoes left. Looking at the ground around him, Asesakes picked up a rock the size of an egg and launched it toward the last canoe. He spun and fell onto the stony beach as he let go.

The rock splashed into the sea, well behind the last canoe. The braves in the canoe did not take notice.

Asesakes got to his knees. *What can I do now?* The Mohegan warriors would come, and there would be no Manissean men to oppose them. *We will all die or be taken as slaves.*

Someone came up behind him. Asesakes turned to see the big, older girl named Alsoomse. He gritted his teeth and shook his head. *"What do you want?"*

She was a handsome girl, just a year younger than Asesakes and was always involving herself in the things of boys and men.

Alsoomse flicked her chin toward the receding war party and declared, "That last canoe, I can reach."

"Ahhhh." Asesakes groaned, "Go away. You are just a *Yôksqáhs!*"

The girl shrugged her shoulders and turned away. But then Asesakes recalled watching her throwing rocks with the boys and being amazed at how hard and how much farther she could throw. He turned and yelled, "Wait! If you are not boasting into the air, *Yôksqáhs*, then do it— now! Quickly!"

Alsoomse slowly looked around, scanning the rocks around her feet.

"Quickly, you, *kôkci citsak!*"

Alsoomse pouted. She picked up a rock and turned it over in her hand, nodding as she tested its weight.

Asesakes pounded the sand crying out, "*kipi!*"— begging her to hurry.

With a slow motion and what seemed little effort, the girl flung the rock high and far out over the water toward the canoes.

Asesakes strained to watch the flight of the rock in the deepening twilight. He lost sight of the stone but then saw the last brave in the last canoe jerk before hearing a distant, crisp smack as the rock hit something hard. The last brave slumped over to upset the canoe balance. It rolled on its side swamping the men and their weapons.

Asesakes winced and looked over at Alsoomse, whose white teeth were glowing within her open smile. She proudly nodded her head.

"Alsoomse, you have done well, but our men may return with angry blows for this. Go to the village. I will say I threw rock."

The girl's smile disappeared, "No, I will stay."

"Please!" Asesakes begged. "I do not want your blood on my *nicish.*"

Alsoomse stared back. "You will repay me for this one day."

"*Nuks!*" He waved his hand, "Now go!"

Alsoomse's eyes flared and she bared her shiny teeth. "I do not take instruction from you." She turned and ran off.

Asesakes looked back out to the canoes. The commotion from the swamped canoe attracted the attention of the other braves. They turned their canoes to come to the aid of the men in the water.

Gathering a bundle of dry sea grass, Asesakes ran toward the smoldering fire. He blew on the ashes until he had a glowing coal and then set the grass afire. Some of the women there followed suit. They waved their improvised torches. Asesakes cupped his hands and screamed another *wôpsukuhq* eagle cry.

Faces in the canoes began looking back toward shore. He waved his arms and continued yelling. When one canoe turned back the others aimed their prows toward the beach. Asesakes drew a deep breath. The knot in his stomach released but he grabbed his belly as it rumbled. Its contents of seal fat erupted and Asesakes vomited. The young brave sighed and wiped his mouth. He felt better and nodded, *That was a good yakus pakitam.*

~~~

Sachem Jacquantu was in the first canoe to reach the beach, and Asesakes was there at the water's edge to meet him.

"There are many canoes coming. Not from Montauk but from Quinnehtukqut." Asesakes called out.

"How many?" Jacquantu asked.

"They were far. But by splashing paddles, five to six canoes."

The Sachem looked away in thought. He answered, "Before highest moon they will land." The old man's face grew stern. "We have much to do. Mohegans plan to surprise us." He then smiled a sparsely toothy grin. "But, we will surprise the Mohegans."

The remaining Manissean canoes were coming back to shore. The canoe that had swamped was the last to arrive. Those men were wet and angry. They dragged the unconscious brave out of the canoe, over the rocks and onto the beach. He groaned and held his head.

"*Mikucut!*" Asesakes cursed. It was Audsah.

Asesakes looked up to the sky and bit his lip. Of all the people on Manisses Island, Audsah was the last one Asesakes would want to anger. He was big and strong, and he was always looking to fight.

"What happened?" The sachem called to the wet men. "Did you fall over catching that big fish?"

"No, something fell from the sky." The men seemed in no mood for humor. "It hit Audsah on the head. He has large lump and bleeds."

The sachem laughed. "More like you hit him on the head with a paddle." He then called out to all the braves gathering on the beach, "Do not be angry. That we returned is good. Asesakes spotted canoes from the mainland—Mohegans from Quinnehtukqut. We will be ready. They will wish they never came back to Manisses." He waved a hand toward the canoes. "Clear your *muhshoyash* from the beach. Then we all gather to make for the Mohegan's great surprise."

Asesakes' chest swelled and he lifted his chin high. It was his name being called out for bringing about this chance for a great victory. Several of the older *Inak* braves looked at him, nodding their heads in approval. Others slapped him on the back or chest as they passed by to acknowledge their favor.

I am now one of the Inak—a warrior! The boy grinned.

Asesakes nodded to the women and children who smiled back at him. He turned to look down the beach and met Audsah's gaze. His smile drooped. The hair on his neck bristled. The angry brave sat on the beach rubbing his head and staring at him. The scowl on Audsah's face spoke many words. The boy was certain Audsah knew that Asesakes had something to do with his pain and embarrassment.

The boy's stomach rumbled again. Of this he was also certain; the proud brave will get his revenge.

Chapter 2

The Manisseans

"Uncas has broken from the Pequots." Sachem Jacquantu called out. "His Mohegans will make their own land and people. They have taken villages on Montauk and seek to take us from our Narragansett brothers but Manisses they will not have!"

The braves screamed *wôpsukuhq* cries. The sachem waved his hands to quiet them. "Where these wolves will land, we know," He pointed south, "at the *Wôkáyu icuk* of the west beach."

The sachem poked his war club into the sand. "Mohegans carry a spirit believing they have already won. What defeats them will be this spirit." Once again, the braves erupted into eagle cries. The sachem raised his hand. "This is what we will do. They will beach their canoes, ready for escape. They will move east along the trail inland until the trail turns north toward the waters of our *Muhshaki Nupsapáq* and our summer villages to attack. But, we will meet them with surprises to turn them south away from our villages on the Great Pond and trap them." He picked up his walking stick and pointed east. "Go now to your places!"

~~~

The moon was high in the night sky, casting a bright light across the water. Asesakes peered from his lookout post further to the north to watch the Mohegan canoes approaching the island. He rubbed his hands together. *Our tribe is ready.* Almost every one of his tribe of over one thousand—all but the youngest and the oldest, who were now hidden away—would take part in the plan to trap and kill the Mohegans.

Asesakes watched the Mohegans' progress and just as Jacquantu had said, they headed for the landing on the west beach. He ran off to join the braves in hiding. His heart pounded as he ran through the forests along the narrow trails. He slapped some of the large trees as he ran. It was this thick forest that would act as a great friend and helper to their war party. Manisses, "The Little God" itself, would rise up to be the one to defeat their enemy.

The young brave's chest burned with excitement and fear. The Manisseans were the ones to be surprised by the Mohegans and the Pequots. They could do little more than run and hide, as they had been overrun by their enemy in the past. *Now, we will rise up and fight!* Approaching the west beach, he ran past braves hidden in the trees and bushes along the trail.

Arriving at the opening and ducking into the tall reeds, Asesakes crouched behind the sand dunes. He peaked out to the water; there were the Mohegan dugouts closing on the beach. Yes, it was five canoes with ten men in each boat. The young brave ran while crouching over and found Jacquantu, who was hiding with others south of the west beach trail.

Before he could report, the sachem said, "Good. They are here. Run and call out along the trails to be ready. Just as has been revealed, this will be Manisses' plan. Do not be seen." He pushed the boy toward the trail. "*Kipi!*"

Crouching down below the tall grass and the small dunes as he ran, Asesakes could hear the Mohegans landing on the beach. He bolted into the forest. When he reached the point in the trail that passed between the two tall hills he began repeatedly calling out in a loud whisper, "Mohegans are here. Be ready. Manisses victory!"

He was headed to the other end of the west beach trail where it intersected with the center trail that ran north to south. It was there that Penewess and a large number of their strongest braves would meet the Mohegans and turn them south toward the great jaws of Manisses. To the place they call, *Shwi Wôkáyu Niputash.* Asesakes chuckled and clapped his hands with excitement, *A big surprise we have for you Mohegans. You will run away to the tallest bluffs!*

Once the Mohegans left the beach and their canoes, Jacquantu and the braves at the beach, as well as those hiding along the west beach trail, would first destroy the Mohegan canoes to prevent any escape.

Asesakes' hair on his body bristled with excitement. He pounded his chest. *This will be the first of many great victories!*

He ran. Something caught his ankle and he tumbled over and over down the trail, landing hard on his back. His head was spinning. He gasped as someone jumped on top of him. A large hand clasped his neck. He was choking.

In the streaks of moonlight piercing through the forest, Asesakes saw a hatchet being raised. The young brave grabbed the raised arm. His mind raced, *How can the Mohegans be upon me so quickly? Have we already been discovered?*

The hatchet hovered above him. The brave on his chest growled. Asesakes' eyes came into focus, and he saw the face. It was not a Mohegan; it was Audsah, who seethed through clenched teeth, "You did it." He squeezed tighter on Asesakes' neck. "I know it was you hitting me with a stone to make me look *asoku.*"

"Audsah, no!" Asesakes choked, "Not me."

"If not you, who?"

"It was Manisses, 'The Little God,' to turn you around—to bring you back to save us. What had to be done, Manisses did."

Audsah paused and eased his grip. He slowly brought the hatchet down and slipped the edge under Asesakes' chin. "Now, we need every brave." He growled. "But like a storm that rumbles *patáhqáham* after the flash of *wôwôsôpshá* you will feel my wrath. Only after our fight with Mohegans is *kisi*—over."

Audsah jumped off of him and went back to his hiding place in the forest. Asesakes got up. His head hung low as he continued jogging down the path, rubbing his neck while he called out warnings to the Manisseans to be ready. *Maybe dying by Mohegan hands is better than facing Audsah's wrathful kihcapun?*

Asesakes stopped again. His heart jumped as another figure appeared on the trail in front of him. Fear seized him. *Who is this now?* The fear turned to disgust. It was the difficult girl, Alsoomse! He charged at her and hissed, "What are you doing here?" He shoved her. "Doesn't Jacquantu have a plan for our women?"

"Yes," Alsoomse straightened up, "But I can fight! As good as any brave, I can shoot arrows and throw rocks!"

Asesakes stopped to think, *I cannot argue with that.* He answered, "But the women need your strength for Jacquantu's plan to carry baskets of *kuhthan wunipaqash* to the top of the bluff." He pointed down the trail. "You must go if Manisses will defeat the Mohegans."

She looked away. "I will go but not because you tell me." She trotted off and called over her shoulder. "I will go for Manisses."

Chapter 3

The Mohegans

The slim edge of the large wooden canoe bumped along the gradual incline of sand and stone. Five Mohegan warriors simultaneously leapt from either side of the canoe as if springing into a perfectly choreographed dance. Each of the remaining canoes filled with ten Mohegan warriors landed and performed the same leaping pirouette into the shallow water. They all dragged their canoes well up onto the west side beach and gathered their weapons to encircle one brave who stood a full head above the rest.

Quttajuia was tall and thick. His large head was framed by a square jaw and long, flowing black hair from on top. He was a lower sachem sent by the Mohegan sachem Uncas in Quinnehtukqut to lead this war party to harass the Manisseans.

Next to him stood a smaller and older brave named Mingan—the Gray Wolf. Mingan provided wisdom and counsel to the young sachem.

The powerful sachem addressed his men, "Yes, we come for riches of woven mats, *mosopish*, *suksuwak*, and *wiwáhcumunsh*. This is not our purpose. Our *wáci* is to remind Manisseans that this is Mohegan land—for Mohegans from Quinnehtukqut to have."

The men grunted their affirmation.

Quttajuia continued, "We know well the land around their Great Pond. We will take and they will not fight. They are like frightened *citsak*—weak baby birds."

The men laughed.

Quttajuia put up his hand and hissed, "Quietly we go in. But, like *muksak*—wolves we scare, take what we want and go. For Manisseans this is how it will be." He turned and called, "Come!"

The sachem led the party down the path and into the forest. The path through the dense forest was narrow, not allowing for much more than one man to march through in a single line. The group moved quickly and quietly.

As Quttajuia marched he asked Mingan, "Why is my spirit not more excited to frighten these people?"

"Because they are weak and have no fight." The elder answered

"True. The thought of these weak Indians leaves a taste of bad fish in my mouth." He spat on the ground. "This will be no challenge."

The sachem led his men down the path as they passed between two high hills. His ears pricked up. He stopped. The sound of a broken twig. He scanned the forest. Then another sound. He grinned. *What plans to surprise us do these baby birds have?*

A rustling and then cries of pain came echoing from the rear of the line.

"What happened?" the sachem called back.

Quttajuia's cousin, the young brave named Kitchi reported, "From behind two have been hit with arrows. Not wounded badly."

The braves began to chatter amongst themselves until Quttajuia called out, "Quiet!"

"Ahhh," The sachem spoke in a gravely whisper. "We have been discovered. Our baby birds think they can fight."—and then more loudly, he laughed and said, "*Wikôtamuwôk* we will now have with them." He rubbed his hands together. "This will be fun now. They are weak people who will run and hide when we fight. Come. Move into their summer villages."

The Mohegans began marching forward. An eagle cry sounded from the forest and all kinds of animal sounds erupted. Rocks and arrows and sharp items began showering down from the forest up on the hillsides, pelting the Mohegans. The group ducked down to find cover.

Quttajuia yelled, "Into the trees. Go! Attack them!"

When the braves jumped up to enter the woods, the pelting stopped, and it was quiet again. The sachem stood and looked around but could not see any of their attackers.

A number of the braves were cut and bleeding but none seriously. Quttajuia wondered, *What are your plans?* He chuckled and called out, "So, you think you can fight us?"

Kitchi asked, "Do we go back to the boats?"

Quttajuia's face flushed and his heart raced. He grabbed Kitchi's shoulder, "Of little birds are you afraid?"

He pushed him away. "Like a little mouse will you run away?"

"Quttajuia, there is a different spirit here." Mingan called out. "They are not surprised. Should we return another time to surprise them?"

"Fifty Mohegan warriors we have!" He cried. "When we fight, they will run. Run away we do not!" He stared at the men and they shrank back from his fiery gaze. "Come after me!" He turned and began to run continuing east through the forest. His men followed right behind.

Quttajuia neared the end of the trail and the opening where the forest thinned out. He gathered his men together. "You see how they fight with sticks and stones like *sqahsihsak*—little girls hiding in the forest. I was going to let many live, but now they will know real fear."

He looked out toward the opening. "When we come out of forest they will be waiting for us. With wolf howls we will charge them. They will scatter."

Quttajuia let out a howl that echoed through the forest and swept through the Mohegans. The men rallied and began howling. The Sachem continued to howl as he charged out of the forest and into a clearing of tall grass, with his men massed behind him. He turned up the trail north, ready to throw himself and his men headlong into the Manisseans.

The Mohegans were met with a hail of arrows, but Quttajuia did not slow. An arrow weakly sailed at him, but he knocked it aside with his club. He charged forward and glanced back to beckon his men on.

What? He looked back to find that he was alone. His men were stopped—frozen behind him. He snapped his head back around and gasped. The brave's body tingled and burned as he slid to a stop.

The sachem backpedaled. He cursed, *"Natiak! Nuskinoqat natiak!"*

~~~ The Manisseans ~~~

Sachem Jacquantu looked on as his fifty braves chopped holes into the Mohegan canoes and set them to drift and sink off from the west beach.

Asesakes came running onto the beach and up to Jacquantu. "The *natiak* are ready."

The sachem smiled. His plan—the plan of 'The Island of The Little God' would work. He spoke to the men, "When I first spotted Quttajuia leading the Mohegans, I was uncertain. His work I have seen before. A strong spirit is his."

"Will they turn south toward the great bluffs?" Asesakes asked.

"Not so strong are the other Mohegans." The old sachem reasoned, "If we can get the others to turn, he will go too."

Jacquantu called to his men, "We wait on the beach to see if any Mohegans return to escape by their canoes."

"Do we kill them?" Asesakes asked.

"Quttajuia's pride I know." The sachem shook his head. "I am certain they will not try to flee." He shrugged his shoulders. "If they do, we will see."

27

"Will your plan for Penewess succeed?"

"Where the center trail crosses the trail to west beach Penewess and his men with the *natiak* will be waiting." He chuckled. "The look on the Mohegan's faces I wish to see. Their war cries will turn to *páhpohs* crying for their mothers."

"Why do Mohegans fear the island *natiak?*" Asesakes wondered.

"I am not certain of this. When they have attacked in the past they have always ordered us to kill our *natiak* or tie them up." Jacquantu nodded. "Driving them to destruction will be their fear—their *uyutáháwôk*."

Chapter 4

The Mohegans

A slew of arrows and lances passed around him. Quttajuia stopped and held his ground. He stood up straight and faced the one hundred Manissean men. He reminded himself, *These are only farmers and fishermen. They do not know how to fight. Scaring me, they do not.* He rubbed his chin. *But, what is their new fighting spirit?*

The urge to turn away was taking hold. It was the line of *natiak*. His spirit began to tremble. *I fear nothing*, he told himself. As he backed away, he called out to his men, "Come back and fight. We are warriors! They are not even real men!"

As Quttajuia glanced over his shoulder, a small arrow poked him in his chest. He pulled it out and threw it away. His men hesitated, caught between turning away or charging forward.

The sachem wondered, *What was this thing that caused such fear in his men and even in himself? This thing now lined up in front of the Manisseans?*

He took several steps back and surveyed the thirty island braves lined up front, each wrestling with a long pole, and tied to the end of each pole was one of the frothing, snarling, fearsome island *natiak*—the dogs of Manisses.

The Islanders had the dogs tied and muzzled at the end of each pole with two ropes. When the Mohegans came around the corner, the Manisseans pulled on one rope that released the muzzle from the dogs.

Quttajuia and his men ran into a wall of surprised, angry, snarling, barking, howling, and snapping dogs. It was unexpected and horrifying.

The Mohegans back—peddled in terror.

As the sachem backed away he sized up the threat calling to his men, "They are not big. We can kill them."

Mingan stepped closer and responded, "Yes, but look at them." He pointed at the dogs. "They are powerful!" He stepped behind Quttajuia. "Their short legs, strong chests, heavy rumps and massive jaws filled by sharp teeth can tear a man apart. They are vicious animals that do not back down."

"They are Manissean in their blood!" The Sachem shot back.

"I do not know how these Indians and these dogs live together on this small island." Mingan shouted above the snarling racket, "But, these dogs are nothing like the Manisseans."

Quttajuia backed off. He did not want to, but his men had already turned to go down the trail south. He ordered, "*Ahqi!*"

The men running down the south trail stopped when they realized that the dogs were not chasing them.

The Sachem raised his club and pointed to the dogs, "What do you fear? Our people have fought with only hands and killed wolves, mountain lions, and bears. Why do we fear *natiak*?"

Kitchi stuttered, "Wild *natiak* have spirits of men who could not leave this world and stay angry." He wiped sweat from his brow. "They stay trapped in *natiak*. Anyone could be an enemy we killed now seeking revenge."

"We have killed and eaten dog before!" Quttajuia growled, "We will do the same to them!"

"Yes, but only when there was nothing else to eat." Mingan countered.

As the Mohegans argued, the dogs continued pulling and jumping forward with such power that many were dragging their Indian handlers forward.

Quttajuia yelled, "We will turn and charge them to first kill their dogs and then kill them!"

A cry coming from the Manisseans caused all Mohegan eyes to turn back to the dogs.

The natives yelled, "Attack!" and pulled on the second rope, releasing the dogs. The natiak exploded in snarling rage after the Mohegans.

Quttajuia could not hold his ground. He ran with most of his men escaping away from the attacking dogs, along the trail headed south. A few of his men broke off and took the trail back west trying to escape to their boats.

Along either route, hidden Manissean Indians were pelting the Mohegans with stones and sharp objects. The sachem was confused and disoriented, with only the path south in front of him to escape.

The island dogs were quickly on the Mohegans and snapped at their feet and legs. They pressed on, with some knocked down by rocks that struck them in the head or with sticks or ropes set to trip them.

The enraged dogs immediately overwhelmed the men who fell. Their screams echoed across the island as the dogs ripped and tore into their bodies.

Enough of the Mohegans had fallen that the dogs were fully occupied. Quttajuia had beaten off the dogs with his club. He ran and gathered together with the rest of his war party.

He surveyed the group. "Staying on this trail is too dangerous," he decided. "After me."

When he reached an opening, Quttajuia led them east into an open field—into the soft wet mud and stagnant waters of the island's largest *Mahcáq*.

He sloshed ahead calling out, "Through the swamp the dogs cannot follow."

As the Mohegans slogged slowly through the open space of muddy water and tall grass, rocks and arrows came raining down on them. Quttajuia pressed on, looking for a place where they could make a stand.

The Grey Wolf cried out, "We must get out of this open place!"

The sachem led the band to head southeast. But, every time they turned east or west, a new flurry of objects was hurled at them.

Quttajuia stopped and Mingan counseled, "We must not be the hunted!"

The sachem stepped forward toward the unseen enemy and yelled out, "Stop hiding and come out to fight!" His challenge was met with silence.

He yelled again, "Come out! Like real braves, face us! Real warriors!" This time the response was more rocks and arrows pelting them.

Quttajuia waved his hand toward the nearest high ground with dry, thick forest. The men followed and they huddled together to gather their strength. All looked to their sachem.

Quttajuia asked Mingan, "How many are still with us?" Mingan counted the number of braves and their weapons. He reported, "We arrived with fifty and now have twenty—eight. Only half the men now have weapons."

The sachem looked up into the sky and cursed, "What has happened?"

~~~ The Manisseans ~~~

The sour salt air filled his nostrils. He took several deep breaths to stretch his lungs and settle his nerves. The tide was coming up and the surf, for the west side of the island, was unusually heavy. The waves repeatedly crashed on the stony beach with a deafening roar.

I must hear the dogs. Moving away from the beach, Jacquantu put his hand up to his ear. The other braves quieted and also listened. He relayed, "Inland, I hear the island dogs—howling and attacking the Mohegans." He smiled. The others nodded their heads.

"Some Mohegans might escape this way," He looked into their faces. "but to quit and run would not be like Quttajuia. A few of them may break and come for boats. We will meet them." He pointed to the dunes. "In the grass, we will hide. If all of them come back, we wait for Penewess and his men to come. Then we attack. If it is only a few Mohegans, we charge them."

The men grunted in agreement, and they hiked up into the dunes on both sides of the trail to the west beach. They waited for the Mohegans.

The sachem knelt in the sand and looked at Asesakes. He shook his head. "A fighter I am not. Our people are not trained in fighting and war."

"Audsah is a fighter." Asesakes insisted.

"Yes, but he has spent much time with the Pequot. He has learned to be a 'destroyer' from them."

Asesakes pressed the sachem, "But I have heard stories from the old braves that our people once did fight other tribes. Did you not fight with them?"

The sachem stared down the trail, "I did fight but that was another life. It was long ago. We had to fight to survive." He sighed. "That is why we travelled *akômuk* from the other side, to live in peace on Manisses. It was long before anyone came to trouble us here."

Asesakes shook his fist and in a loud voice said, "We are not a weak people. We are strong."

"Yes." Jacquantu waved his hand to quiet the young brave. He whispered, "Strong are our men but not trained to fight. It has been too long. We have relied on Manisses for protection—our distance from the mainland and from the strength of our Narragansett brothers."

He raised his head to listen and then dropped down to continue, "When the Pequot began to war with the Narragansett, they decided to steal from Manisses."

Asesakes rubbed his chin, "Why did we not fight them when they first came?"

"Then, they only came to prove that they could. They did little harm and did not take much. Not very often did it happen, so we did not resist. Peace was all we wanted."

"But, what made the Mohegans bolder and more terrible?"

"When the Mohegans broke off from the Pequot, they became more violent and took more for themselves. Anyone who fights back, they kill or make slaves." The sachem poked Asesakes with his walking stick. "You remember the last Mohegan war party that came, burning and destroying many homes and crops. It was then that I agreed with Penewess. Our "Island of the Little God" needs to fight—even to attack our enemies. So, I made a plan for war."

The Sachem's ears pricked up. War cries and movement echoed down the trail. A chill swept over him leaving his hair standing on end. He shivered. Every muscle tensed and his heart pounded as the blood surged through his veins. He felt alive and mused, *it has been a long time since I felt this pumôtam with life!*

The Sachem looked around. *Manissean braves have been acting bolder, more confident, and not as fearful.* But, now he looked at the men crouching in the weeds. *They look scared and frightened. Was this a good thing? Could men who grew knowing only farming and fishing become true warriors?* A spirit whisper crept into his mind saying, *This is a mistake. We will be destroyed.*

No! His mind fought back. *This is Manisses' plan and it is working. To survive this is what we must do. It is all happening as the 'Island of the Little God' told me.*

"Mohegans coming this way" He called out to his men in a loud whisper. "escaping to their canoes."

Asesakes' voice quivered, "What if it is all of them? If it is, can we really fight them?"

Jacquantu was not certain. He spoke as if he was, "It will not be all of them. Our people in the forest will be causing whoever is coming great pain. They will be wounded already."

He called out to his men, "Ready to strike as *sihsiqak* snakes! Wait for it!"

The sachem counted them as the Mohegans stumbled from the forest and jogged out to the beach. It was only six and only one was carrying a war club. All were cut and bleeding. He chuckled as they hopelessly searched the beach. He snickered, "Where are your canoes now?"

It was time. Jacquantu yelled, "Now! *Kipi!* Go fast!"

Fifty Manisseans swarmed the beach with their clubs, axes, and hatchets to encircle the six Mohegans.

The Mohegans were dazed. They held up their hands in surrender while one still held his club. Jacquantu felt the eyes of his men on him looking for direction. The sachem stepped forward but hesitated. *What do I do Manisses? Do we show mercy or do we destroy?*

The Islanders began to close their circle waving their weapons in the air, waiting for the order. Then the one Mohegan with a club took a swipe.

The islanders responded. His men leapt upon the six Mohegans. Jacquantu gasped. They savagely hacked and clubbed them.

One Mohegan cried out, "Awán na skitôpak?"

The old sachem stood slack jawed—stunned at the brutality of his men. He shook off his shock and answered the Mohegan, "You ask who we are?" He beat his chest with his fist. "We both know now!"

Chapter 5

The Mohegans

A dull, rhythmic, and persistent drumming of clubs against tree trunks, accented by random screeching cries of *wôpsukuhq* filled the air. The sounds were only an annoyance to Quttajuia but he looked around to see that it was effectively unnerving his men.

The sachem surveyed the tangle of forest surrounding them and looked for counsel from Mingan.

"The island Indians are proving resourceful."

"Yes, they are out there, hidden in thick brush and trees, yet, we cannot see them. Creeping closer and closer."

"I wonder if they are driving us in a certain direction—to a certain place?" Mingan looked south. "But why?"

"This is an island. We will certainly come to a beach, where we will be forced to fight or to swim away."

"I do not know this island well" Mingan conceded, "but maybe we move south quickly until we reach the beach and circle back to our boats."

Kitchi joined them, "Should we split up and move in different directions? The Manisseans may not follow us all."

Quttajuia hesitated as he stared into the sky. He shook his head. "No, we will stay together. Let us move from here. Where they are not, is where we will go." He picked up a large stick. "As we go, look for things to use as weapons. These island people are not fighters. The *natiak* are no longer at our heals. Let us go."

The sachem led his men southwest through the forest. But, once again, whenever they tried to turn to the east or to the west, they were driven to continue south.

Quttajuia began to move faster and then broke into a run, calling to his men, "Follow me, quickly. *Kipi!*"

The frustration rose up and pounded in his head. His anger began to burn in his chest. He cracked his club against the trees as he ran. *Who are these people? Was this really a battle they could win?* His thoughts turned to outrunning his pursuers; to make their way back to the boats and to Quinnehtukqut. *No more of this new Manissean spirit!* He spotted an opening and called to his men, "Up ahead in the clearing. This is where we will turn back north and go back to the boats."

Quttajuia broke out of the forest. He glanced north and then south. *Yes, the trail is clear!* His men followed him out of the forest and at the very same time two large groups of Manissean braves, also broke out of the forest onto the wide trail, just fifty paces to the north and fifty paces to the south of the Mohegans.

The drumming stopped. The war parties stood silently looking at one another. Quttajuia chewed on his lip and flexed his shoulders. This was his first good look at the island Indians since they had landed. They were what he had remembered; tall, slim, not at all impressive. He was not intimidated. This was not a group that looked eager to fight. He saw fear.

There, out front, stood a young, lanky brave. The Mohegan sneered and growled at the pup. The boy shook and stumbled a step back.

Quttajuia made up his mind. *We will charge and fight through the Manisseans to the north.* He took a step toward them but several of his own braves bolted back into the forest to avoid the confrontation. The sachem yelled "*áhqi!*" to stop them but the rest of his men followed the others. He pounded his club into his hand. *I cannot fight them alone!*

He stared into the boy's eyes like a wolf would stare at the frightened prey he was about to devour. *You will die at my hands you little ayumohs.*

He bolted to follow his men and cursed as he ran. *By so weak a foe, how can we be pushed around? Face-to-face we must fight them. And that boy—that fearful little Manissean pup, I will make a point to destroy him myself for thinking he could stand up to a Mohegan warrior!*

~~~ The Manisseans ~~~

The trees in the forest began to spin. Asesakes' heart pounded as he ran from the west beach. He stopped to catch his breath and to wipe the moisture from his face. He looked at his hands. They were red. It was not sweat but

Mohegan blood covering his face and arms. He bent over and vomited.

The young brave's mind was full of what had just happened; replaying it all in his head. His first taste of a battle with an enemy. The images of his club coming down on another man's head, hearing the crack of the bones and feeling his club's bruising contact with flesh, followed by the warmth of the blood splattering his skin. It drove him wild with excitement and it made him sick once again.

The young brave gasped for air as he joined with Penewess' men moving to the north of the Mohegan's position. They were driving them to the southeast. The attack on the beach was their first victory. Still, he felt weak. *Could it be true? Could their plan be really working?*

The island dogs had caught and torn to pieces eight of the Mohegans. Those who were left alive by the dogs were finished off with clubs. Others were chased into the great swamp, where they tired and became easier targets to shoot arrows and throw things at. Now, they were through the swamp and hiding in the forest on the other side.

A new spirit had come upon his tribe. All were strengthened by this spirit. It caused them to have the courage to fight like never before. Asesakes pondered, *We Manisseans are good humans, but Mohegans are not. To protect ourselves, we need to fight like Mohegans.*

Audsah was one of the few in the tribe who was a fighter. He was never liked for that, but for now, he was glad that Audsah was part of his war party. Whenever the

Mohegans tried to break to head north, Audsah was the one who would lead the fight to drive them back southeast.

So, is this new spirit of their tribe a woonanit—good spirit or a mattanit—bad spirit? Asesakes wondered. He had never been taught that fighting and warring were good things but now they were. Now, the pleasure he felt from the beating of their enemy confused him. The uncertainty began to gnaw away his courage.

The young brave was jolted from his thoughts as Penewess called out, "Let us move!" The Mohegans were on the move again, and his group ran to keep ahead of them. The Manisseans had an advantage, in that they knew the terrain and every rock, bush, and tree of their small island.

Penewess called to him, "Asesakes, take the lead and keep an eye to where they are headed." The boy's chest swelled once more. He took off but then slowed as he thought, *If we stumble into them and they attack what will I do? I will be crushed.*

He told himself, *I must not lose track of them!* His heart stopped and panic grabbed hold as his eyes darted about. *Where did they go?* He moved faster to locate their enemy now lost in the shadowy moonlight.

Asesakes bolted out onto the wide trail. He froze. *There they are.* Nothing between them. The other braves in his party came out onto the trail behind him. He held his breath as his whole body shook.

Here he was face to face, not more than fifty feet from the imposing Mohegan Sachem. There were no dogs or forest for protection. The Sachem glared straight into his eyes and the evil gaze was enough to make Asesakes stumble back as if he had been shoved.

The Mohegans were going to charge and kill them all. Of this Asesakes was now certain. He held his breath and braced for the charge. Then the young brave's jaw dropped. He slowly exhaled as he watched the Mohegans, inexplicably, retreat back into the forest.

Chapter 6

The Mohegans

"You are not warriors! You act as scared little girls!" Quttajuia yelled. He pounded his club against a rock. "We could have driven right through those weak Islanders. Made our way back north—back to the boats."

"But they have a new spirit about them." Mingan answered. "It is not them, it is their spirit."

"No other choice do we have?" The sachem rubbed the back of his neck. "Continue south until we reach the sea." He declared, "We will make our way back from there."

"Follow me." Quttajuia ran. He scanned the forest. The Manisseans continued chasing them on either side. The ground was becoming steeper, and soon he was hiking up a steady incline. He reached the top of the hill that cleared the trees. He stopped and surveyed the area. Quttajuia took a long breath and called out, "The Islanders have given up chasing us!" His men gathered around him.

From this vantage point, Quttajuia looked back north to see much of the island. The moon was now dropping low but still shone brightly. He could make out Quinnehtukqut, from where they had come. To the west was the shadowy landform of Montauk. The low moon was illuminating a swath of light across the great sea.

"Do you think they have given up on us?" Kitchi asked

"No, Manisseans are still watching us, preparing for what is next." The sachem growled and pounded his fist to his chest. *These people I have considered too lowly*, he thought. *Was it true? Was a new Island spirit fighting for them?*

Quttajuia looked into the sky gauging the time. *The sun will soon be rising.* He looked over his men who rested against the rocks. *I too will rest.* He sat on a rock and let the tension in his shoulders release, allowing himself the time to soak in the surroundings of the land. With the moon shadows and the hilly terrain, the land looked more like a rolling sea with hills and valleys dotted by many small shinning ponds and lakes. To the north were large fields for planting. Many of these fields they had burned in the past. It was a waste but something that needed to be done to keep the Islanders weak and afraid.

The powerful Sachem let himself imagine living a quiet, peaceful life, separated from others on the mainland. *Perhaps one day, when I am old, I will take the island as my own.* He let himself smile and wondered, *Do I regret spoiling this life for the Manisseans?* He shook off the notion. *No, these are weak people who do not deserve this land.*

Quttajuia stood back up to survey their situation and size up where to move next. He peered into the night shadows of the forest. He could see the Manisseans moving in the woods, encircling them from the north, east, and west. *Gathering in the forest around us is the whole Manissean tribe.* The Sachem had always believed that he could overcome any difficulty and any foe. He ground his teeth and rapped his forehead. *I was not prepared for this!* He hung his head. Doubt seeped in. *Will we be able to go back to my people in Quinnehtukqut?*

The Sachem called the braves together. "Come, you *Kôkci ohqák* maggots." His men laughed and circled around him. "This seems a safe place, but it is not."

"Is this not good ground to fight?" Kitchi spoke. "It is high, and the Manisseans will have to charge from the forest up the hill to fight us. We should make this the place to fight."

He waved him off. "No. We have only a few weapons." The sachem grimaced. "There is nothing here for us to eat or drink. They can wait on us. Before they complete to circle around us, we must keep moving."

Quttajuia had his doubts. He would not let it show. "There are many of these island people out there, but they cannot fight." He raised his club up in the air. "We are Mohegan warriors. Weak and afraid are these people. They have yet to fight us brave-to-brave. We will fight our way to the boats and return to Quinnehtukqut. Then we will come back, and they will want to die before they face us again." He pointed his club south. "Go! Make our way to the beach."

The Mohegan braves began bellowing and howling wolf cries. The whole forest around them responded with eagle cries and the pounding of trees, silencing the Mohegan's wolf cries. Quttajuia waved for them to follow him and they hiked out of the rocks, trotting south along a foot path.

At a low point in the path, they came across a marshy, murky pool of water filled with leaves and decaying matter. The men waded in and began to drink. Mingan advised, "This water is not good to drink."

The sachem agreed, "I sense danger here."

A rustling in the bushes to their left spooked them. The braves circled together, and Quttajuia called out, "Come out and face us!"

Out of the brush bounded two snarling island dogs. Quttajuia's heart jumped. The dogs stopped and hesitated for a moment but then attacked. Several braves bolted running through the shallow water. Quttajuia yelled for them, "*Ahqi!*"

The two men kept moving and within a few steps they found themselves sinking to their waists in thick, mucky debris. As the other Mohegans fought off the dogs the two men struggled to get free. They continued to slowly sink into the dark sludge.

Quttajuia swung at the dogs even as he stretched to reach his men. The two men thrashed and grabbed at the vegetation around them to free themselves but continued to sink. Quttajuia drove the dog off of him and turned to reach for his men, now with only their chins above the sludge and arms thrashing to grab onto anything to stop them from sinking.

Screams from the men now pinned to the ground by the dog's powerful jaws locked on each Indian's neck caused Quttajuia to turn back to them. The braves clubbed the dogs but it seemed to have little effect. Then a distant whistle sounded. The dogs released and ran off.

The sachem turned back to the muddy pool where the two braves had been struggling. He gasped. The only sign of them was gurgling ripples from the thrashing going on below.

Kitchi began to head into the water to attempt a rescue but, Mingan called out, "No! You cannot save them. It is a deep peat hole. They are *kisi*—gone. We must move."

~~~ The Manisseans ~~~

The massive face of the powerful Mohegan warrior hung before him – sneering and haunting Asesakes' mind. Even as he continued to lead the way for the group from his tribe, the fear of engaging the Mohegan Sachem caused his body to tremble. Why am I so *wisôsu*? He ran even as his legs shook. *Might I just fall down, unable to move from this fear?*

A shove came from behind. Asesakes fell to the ground. He curled up into a ball trembling, *This is it. With a Mohegan's club, it will all end.* The blow did not come. He peaked through his shaking hands. "Ahhhh!" he cried as he felt the sting from a slap to his head.

It was Audsah. "What is wrong with you, you scared little worm? Like a frightened little *páhpohs* you cringed in fear in front of the Mohegans. You better fear me! If you do not fight, I will kill you!"

Penewess arrived and stood over him. "Enough! To the Mohegans show your fight. We must not let them turn north. Get up Asesakes." He turned to Audsah, "You take the lead and Asesakes, you follow in back."

Asesakes felt his face flush. *I have failed.* He got up and trotted behind the others. *Why am I so fearful?* His people were many and the Mohegans were only a few. Jacquantu was a smart sachem, and his plan with Manisses was working.

His eyes watered. *I just do not want to die.* He loved his island home and did not want to go to another life. He had watched the burials of many of his people, always buried standing up and walking. *Our dead search forever, never to find a home for rest.* He shivered at the thought.

The young brave trotted on in the rear letting the others move ahead. *Why must I fight and die?* He stopped for a moment as if someone was reminding him of the answer. It was not as it was with Audsah, who just wanted to fight. *Manisses and my people I love. To protect what we have, I fight; otherwise, it will be taken away.*

He asked himself, *For this am I willing to die?* He knew the answer. The shaking from the fear that gripped him faded. He wiped his eyes and ran ahead to catch up with the group. The young brave wanted to see Manisses' plan unfold.

The group followed the Mohegans up the long slope to one of the highest points on the island. When they broke through the forest and climbed to the top, Penewess' group from the north met up with Jacquantu's group from the west.

Gathering all his men, Jacquantu spoke. "Runners, go now!" He ordered. "Tell all of our people it is time to gather together in the forest at the Southeast's tallest hill. The only place they can go is to the bluffs." He pointed to Penewess. "Take your men and split them up to circle around on either side to meet the Mohegans east and west of the south rim trail. You will drive them to *Shwi Wôkáyu Niputash*—their final destination."

The old man's voice was growing weak but he screeched out an eagle cry and called out, "Let us hurry to finish them. Go quickly!"

Chapter 7

The Mohegans

The Grey Wolf approached Quttajuia, "Twenty braves remain—all with wounds and most with no weapons." The group jogged past them moving south on the foot path.

Quttajuia wiped the sweat from his brow and shook his head still asking himself, *How could this happen?*

"Maybe it has always been too easy?" Mingan reasoned.

Quttajuia stared back at Mingan wondering, *Does he know my thoughts?* He admitted, "Yes, maybe we have been rocked to sleep like a *páhpohs*."

The sachem scratched his head, "What new spirit is this? Where has it come from?"

"They are clever people in ways that they live." Mingan mused. "We have known that. New ways of farming and fishing and clamming in great amounts." He shrugged his shoulders. "Should we be surprised that they become clever in war?"

"What do you believe is their plan?"

"I do not know. But when we reach water, we will escape."

They came to the top of a rise just as the dawn broke, and Kitchi pointed toward the ocean calling out, "The great *kuhthan* before us!"

Through the trees Quttajuia could now see specks of blue ocean. The group broke into a run descending from the high ground. As they ran, Quttajuia wondered about the distance to the ocean. They had climbed to high ground and now, with the ocean seemingly so close, he wondered, *When we reach shore, what will we find?*

The Mohegans stepped out onto the next trail that crossed the island's south end from east to west. They were met with a shower of arrows from the west. Quttajuia ducked down as the man next to him took an arrow through the neck and dropped, writhing and choking.

Quttajuia was determined to push forward but there were thick, thorn bushes in front of them. He did not hesitate and turned east on the trail, looking for an opening to continue moving toward the water. A large party of the island Indians appeared farther east down the trail just as Quttajuia spotted an opening ahead of them. The Manisseans let fly another barrage of arrows striking more of the Mohegans. The sachem led the remaining braves onto the trail south. Quttajuia cried out, "To *kuhthan* waters and our escape!"

The crash of heavy surf grew louder. Yet, it sounded strangely distant. The salty, sour odor of low tide struck his nostrils. The forest was opening but there was something wrong. He slowed. Three of his men passed by him and continued to run on. He called out, "Stop!"

The men broke into the clearing and immediately tried to dig their heels in to stop but their forward momentum caused them to slide. They dropped to their knees and clawed at the rippling bed of slimy groundcover. The only thing to grab onto was the loose, wet brown vegetation spread over the top of the bluff.

Quttajuia stood stunned as he watched the three men disappear from sight, leaving only their fading screams as they fell. He held the rest of the men back.

"What is this?" The sachem crept out onto the shiny surface and slipped, nearly falling. He cursed and yelled, *"Kuhthan wunipaqash!"*

Mingan stepped up from behind him. "They have spread their wet seaweed to cause us to slide off the edge." He shook his head in disbelief. "These people are resourceful. All of their island they use against us."

Cautiously wading through the slippery seaweed, Quttajuia pushed it aside with his club. The others followed behind him. He made his way closer to the top of the bluff, struggling to comprehend. *How did they do this?* He looked out. The sun now shone brightly creating a blinding light off the ocean. The sachem shaded his eyes.

He crept closer to the edge and looked over. His men's bodies were splayed, bloodied and lifeless over the rocks far below. He drew a deep breath and stepped back. A strange, calm spirit swept over him. The sense of danger around him seemed to fade. He took in what was now attacking his senses—the brilliant golden sun, alighting the robin's egg blue sky, the vast deeper blue green ocean all seemed something from a dream. He looked over and there were brilliant pink wild beach rose lining the majestic cliffs. It all gave him the sense that he was floating over the endless expanse of ocean. The sun was warm but the air was cool and the sound of the roaring surf below was sweeping his awareness of the danger away.

Quttajuia stepped over to the near bush and picked off a rose. He turned it in his fingers as he scanned the beautiful vista and whispered, "This is why they fight—for this treasure."

Chapter 8

The Manisseans

His feet hurt. The old sachem had fallen behind. Pain
knifed through the arches of Jacquantu's feet, stabbing him
when he stood on them for too long. His people, young and
old, ran past him. He hobbled on. Some would slow out of
respect but he kept encouraging them to hurry and move
more quickly, *"Mômôci! Cáyhqatum!"*

Jacquantu wanted to make certain that their enemy
was driven to the tallest bluff and that they would be
sufficiently surrounded. The whole tribe was to be there to
see that there could be no escape. His people would trap
these Mohegans. *Their Sachem, Quttajuia, has been asoku.
His stupid pride made him think we would never fight back.*

Asesakes came running up to Jacquantu reporting,
"The Mohegans have been turned toward the bluffs."

Jacquantu stopped and leaned against a tree, lifting a
leg to provide one foot some relief. "To the center of *Shwi
Wôkáyu Niputash?*"

"Yes, to the tallest and steepest bluff of her Three
Jagged Teeth."

"Good. That is one where the ground leaves nowhere
to put a foot to climb down." He raised his bushy

eyebrows. "We have a good surprise waiting for them there."

"Do you think our women have completed what you put them to?"

"It is done. They have carried baskets of fresh seaweed up the trail from Stony Beach. It now covers the entire top edge of the bluff."

"But, how are they keeping it wet and slippery?"

"They are using water from the nearby pond." He laughed. "They are ready and we will see if wolves can fly."

"But, for those who don't fly," Asesakes' voice quivered, "will they turn and fight us?"

"It leaves them with no place to hide and nowhere to go. They must fight a thousand men and women to escape." Jacquantu pounded his walking stick on the ground. "Manisses will destroy these Mohegans."

Jacquantu's ears pricked to the sounds farther down the trail. He heard the war cries from his men driving the Mohegans down the final trail to the center bluff. He hobbled forward.

Why don't you rest your feet here?" Asesakes advised.

"No!" Jacquantu shot back, "With my own eyes I want to see fear across Mohegan faces. We have always shown fear; now, we will make the Mohegans *kihcapun*."

"Then what? What next do we do?"

"Hmmm." The sachem shrugged. "Beyond trapping them on bluff, I do not have a plan."

"Do we attack to kill?" Asesakes wondered. "Do we capture them and throw them off? Or, do we just chuck more rocks and shoot more arrows at them?"

"No. This will be Manisses' plan and the 'Island of the Little God's fight. Mohegans fearing to ever coming to Manisses again is what we want." Jacquantu pointed to the sky. "I will wait for instruction from Manisses. Wait until it is clear."

Asesakes ran ahead. The sachem arrived at the trail along the southern rim and moved east. The young brave returned to report, "Our people are all in place. They will not escape."

Jacquantu let out an eagle cry and a slow wave of chanting, *eagle* cries and drumming began to swell up from his people. It grew louder and louder as the full throng of Manisseans joined in. Jacquantu grinned. *The Mohegans are trapped, and my people are letting them hear their victory song!*

He hobbled up the trail to the bluff that lay to the east of where the Mohegans were encircled. He came to the edge and looked across. *There they are huddled together out on the middle bluff. Nowhere to go! Nowhere to hide!*

The 'fearless' Mohegan warriors were crouching down as if struggling to keep the force of the sound from sweeping them off the two-hundred-foot bluff. A surge of emotion bubbled up from deep inside Jacquantu. *Now they know what they do to us.* The old man's emotion erupted and he hollered out, "How does it *uyutáhá*? Do you like how it feels?"

~~~ The Mohegans ~~~

Cautiously, Quttajuia walked to the edge of the bluff. The others joined him to peer over. He called down to the bodies of his men below. They did not respond.

The sachem snapped his head around to a strange sound. It was a soft hum that slowly gathered strength growing louder erupting into a roar. He looked around for its source but it was coming from the west and the east and from the forest to the north.

Mingan spoke, "We are in great danger here."

Quttajuia peeked back over the edge. There was nowhere to climb to escape down to the beach. The woods behind them were filled with hundreds of Manissean braves and their wild dogs. On the bluffs to the left and right, out in the open were the rest of the tribe, cursing and jeering at them.

The sachem called his men together, and they crouched down as Quttajuia spoke over the sound of the crowd. "Escape has only one way—back through the forest. We must fight these people. They have not been tested, and true warriors we know they are not. When we fight them, they will run, and back to our boats we can outrun them."

The sachem looked over his men who were nodding their heads in agreement. But Mingan, shook his head, "This plan I do not think will work. We must climb down to the beach."

His frustration and confusion boiled over. Hot anger shot through Quttajuia's body. He jumped up and stood over the older brave. "You have many years of wisdom but I will decide." *If it were anyone else I would have clubbed you.* "We rest now and gather our strength, then we—" his words were cut off with a thud that knocked one of the men to the ground.

Then the rain came. It was not a wet rain but a rain of rock. The islanders from the bluffs to the east and west began bombarding them with stones. Most of the rocks were being thrown but some braves had slings to reach greater distance. Many stones fell short but enough rocks were hitting among them. They were fully exposed.

Quttajuia began to mock the Manisseans. "Look at these people—they can only fight from a distance with rocks and—" Again he was cut off but this time by a host of arrows coming from the woods and zipping through them. Several of his men were struck and cried out in pain. The Manissean people were lined up along the edge of the bluffs on either side, as if watching a sporting event. They roared with every strike of a rock or an arrow.

Quttajuia yelled, "Dig! We must dig a trench to protect ourselves until we are ready to move."

The Mohegans began to dig with their weapons and hands to pile up the dirt and sand. The arrows stopped, but the rocks continued to sporadically drop down on them. Occasionally, one of his men would hurl the rocks back at the island Indians.

The Mohegans worked through the day and into the night while the Manisseans built fires and camped. His men were growing hungry and thirsty. They had trained themselves to go a long time without eating or drinking. But, their hunger and thirst was made worse as smoke wafted over, with the smell of fish and game cooking on the Manisseans' open fires. The islanders made a show of their food, holding their meat out and splashing their water to be seen clearly by the Mohegans.

Quttajuia tried to distract his men with building the earthworks.

He looked over their work and remarked. "The mound is tall enough to give us protection."

"Yes, but we are still trapped." Mingan added. "You must do something."

The sachem scanned the forest. "I will see if there is a weakness in their defense by sending men out."

Several men tried to sneak into the forest, but each time they did the Manisseans drove them back into their trench with a slew of arrows.

Quttajuia pounded the dirt but then lay back against the earthworks, "Let us rest and gather our strength for tomorrow."

~~~~~~~

By the morning, most of the remaining men, including Quttajuia, were cut and bruised from thrown rocks and arrows.

"Our men grow tired and restless." Mingan exclaimed.

"These people have more fight than I believed." The sachem looked to the Grey Wolf for his help. "What is your plan?"

"Climbing down may be our only way to escape."

Quttajuia nodded "Yes. When sun goes down we will help each other to climb down the bluff to escape."

The sachem informed the men of their plan and they waited until that evening. When it was dark several men held the legs of another man over the edge of the bluff while another climbed down. Another man then climbed down the human rope until he could drop a short distance onto a ledge in the bluff. Once that man stabilized himself on the bluff, he would help the others to climb down.

The plan looked to be working until the man climbing down the human rope slipped from the grasp of the holder. He screamed as he tumbled down the bluff, and then slammed into a boulder. The Manisseans awoke to the Mohegans' attempt to escape and again started raining stones and arrows on them until they retreated back to their trench.

Quttajuia felt all the eyes of his men looking to him for an answer. He slumped against the earthen trench with the others.

Mingan whispered, "Another plan you must come up with quickly."

Quttajuia glared at Mingan and cursed. He spoke to all, "We will wait for now, but later we will charge into forest and capture some of their men. Using them as shields we will make our way back to the boats."

61

Kitchi jumped up, "How long do we wait? We grow weaker. We need to go, now!"

The blood surged to the sachem's face. He grabbed his club to silence Kitchi's disrespect when he heard some odd sounds on the other side of the mound. *What is that?* It did not sound like rocks but thuds of something thrown and hitting the ground.

Quttajuia peeked over the mound. His eyes widened. He felt his stomach growl and his mouth began to water. The others also looked out. There, out in front to of them lay large chunks of cooked meat and fish.

"What are they doing?" Mingan wondered.

Quttajuia scanned to his right and to his left; the bluffs on either side were quiet.

Kitchi said, "They are showing kindness. It is good. I am going." He and another brave crawled out of the earthen fort.

Quttajuia saw some rustling in the bushes. He called out, "Wait! It is a trick."

The men were out of the trench but stopped. No rocks or arrows came.

They ran over to the food and began scooping it up and eating some as they collected it. Kitchi looked back and smiled calling out, "It is good. *Wihpqat!*" He threw some back to the others in the trench.

Thrashing erupted from the forest as another pack of the wild island dogs bolted from the trees, snarling and howling. The animals pounced on the two men, taking them to the ground before they had a chance to move.

More dogs charged past the two and attacked the men in the trench who had caught some of the meats. The men scrambled out of the backside of the earthen fort to the edge of the bluff. The dogs' powerful jaws clamped onto hands and feet, causing those men to stumble backwards and fall off the bluffs, taking the dogs with them.

Now, the only dogs remaining were tearing at the screaming men in front of them. Quttajuia jumped out of the trench to rescue his young cousin, Kitchi. The others also jumped out of the fort to beat off the dogs. At the sound of a whistle the dogs released and ran off back into the forest.

With all of the men out of their fort, the hail of rocks and the arrows came again. Every man was hit with rocks, and many were struck with arrows. Even as they dragged the two mangled men to the trench, several more were knocked unconscious. Those who were still able jumped back into their trench.

Quttajuia leapt back over the earthen wall and felt a burning punch to his back. He looked down to see an arrowhead protruding from his shoulder. Crouching in the trench behind the mound, he looked over his braves. There were now only ten wounded men. His cousin Kitchi was all torn and covered in blood.

He grimaced as he reached around to his back shoulder and snapped off the tail of the exposed arrow. Searing pain shot through his body. He collapsed back against the dirt to rest and then slowly pulled the remainder of the arrow shaft free.

The humming sound began once again and grew louder, surrounding them. "The Manissean victory roar I will not listen to any more!" Quttajuia spoke to Mingan lying next to him. "I will go now to attack these people and fight them where they stand!"

Quttajuia looked around. The rain of rock and arrows ceased, but the moaning of the wounded Mohegans continued. He turned to speak to Mingan and gasped. *No!* He could not breath, feeling as though someone had kicked him in the stomach. The Gray Wolf lay still with an arrow pierced through his temple.

Chapter 9

The Manisseans

Pinching his forefinger and thumb onto the arrow's tail Asesakes slowly pulled back the string of his bow. He looked down the twisted shaft and locked his elbow waiting for the signal. *Penewess' plan to draw Mohegans out with food and then to send in dogs is a good plan. Will it bring all of Mohegans out into the open?*

The young brave could see through the trees and the brush, right to the front of the Mohegans' trench. The dogs were now mauling two of their braves who had come out for the food. Asesakes held back the urge to let his arrow fly into one of them. Then, just as Penewess had planned, the rest of the Mohegans came out to rescue their men from the dogs.

The Manissean sachem gave the order, "*Iyo!*" and the tribe, armed with arrows and rocks, let fly. The ordinance came down as if a huge bucket of water had been turned over on top of the Mohegans. As Asesakes pulled another arrow from his quiver, a second row of their men stepped forward and let their arrows fly. The *yôkôpák* older boys were dispersed among the men and continued to hurl rocks.

The second group stepped back. Asesakes muscles tensed as he stepped forward again to shoot another arrow. His eyes widened as he followed its path. The Mohegans were pulling their men back into the trench. He saw his arrow sink into a Mohegan's shoulder. He pumped his fist. Then he grimaced and felt a sick feeling twist his stomach realizing who it was. It was the shoulder of the large Mohegan sachem. Asesakes' arrow had struck him just before he dropped behind the dirt mound.

The fighting stopped, and there was quiet. Asesakes felt faint. He shrank behind the tree. His body shook, and the fear returned. The young Manissean had wounded the powerful Mohegan sachem who had struck fear into him back on the center trail. *Why do I not feel excited?* He was not. A spirit inside him said that this warrior had set his eye on him—to kill him. *Would his arrow only be like poking a lying natiak with a stick?*

The Manisseans around him began to chant, and the chant swept across the tribe, rising up into a continuous victory cry. Only Asesakes stayed quiet. He stared at the ground, wondering, *where will I escape if the warrior comes after me?*

A kick jabbed him in the leg. Again, he cried out and curled up into a ball, *This is certainly it! The Mohegan is here to kill me!*

The blow did not come, and he heard a familiar angry voice growl, "Get up, you *wisôsu kôcuci ohq mikucut.*"

It was Audsah. Asesakes began to cry, partly from relief but also from embarrassment.

Audsah grabbed his arm and pulled him up, yelling. "Get up! Stop acting like a *páhpohs*. These Mohegans are all wounded and dying. They are finished—*kisi*! I have been begging the sachems to let us end it, but they say no."

Asesakes stood and wiped his face.

"Take your bow and be ready." Audsah shoved Asesakes' bow into the young brave's chest. "If not for them, then for me. When they are done, I will come after you—you and that fat *Yôksqáhs* for hitting me with a rock."

Asesakes body shook. He stared at Audsah who glared back at him while backing away into the forest.

~~~

The tree was thick; the biggest he could hide behind. Asesakes looked up through the trees into the night sky. This night was a long one. He felt trapped and prayed for the daylight to come. *I thought fighting as a warrior would make me a man. But, even now, I feel less.* He took a deep breath. His shoulders slumped. *I have done well to earn a Manissean victory. But, in my spirit there is no hope. If the powerful Mohegan does not kill me, then one of my own will.*

The stars shone brightly through the forest canopy. He fixed his eyes on the brightest star and quietly chanted to Manisses, his 'Island of the Little God' hoping that a great spirit might intervene and give him hope.

Noise and commotion coming from the bluff startled him. His knees shook as he peaked around the tree. Men from his tribe ran past him, fearfully yelling for the others to run as they escaped away from the bluff. Asesakes stumbled out into the trail to see what was happening and his heart stopped.

There on the path was the large Mohegan sachem. Several Manisseans lay dead at his feet. Now, he held another by the neck as he delivered a deathblow to the head with his terrible club. He bellowed out a course wolf howl that echoed through the forest, causing all in the forest to scatter for their lives.

Asesakes froze. His heart somersaulted into his throat. His eyes stayed fixed on the Mohegan. The sachem turned and set his penetrating eyes, red with fire, directly on Asesakes. Now the young Manissean was certain that this was not just a man but an evil spirit. He wanted to run, but he could not move his feet. The Mohegan gaze was fixed as he slowly moved toward him.

Grab an arrow! Asesakes willed his trembling hand to reach for an arrow. He fumbled, notching it in his bow. There was no strength in his arms as he drew back on the bowstring. It was barely drawn when it slipped from his fingers. *No!* He watched as the arrow weakly sailed at the Mohegan, who swatted it away.

Asesakes grabbed for another arrow, but the giant Mohegan was on him, grabbing him by the throat and slowly raising up his other arm with the war club. The young Manissean choked, ready to accept his fate and take the blow. He had no hope.

The Mohegan hissed, "You are not warriors. You are weak. My spirit will return to kill every one of you."

Asesakes was paralyzed by the Mohegan's power. He dumbly nodded. What the evil spirit said rang true. He now would be one of many of this Mohegan's vengeful wrath.

Asesakes laid his head back. His eyes widened as he watched the Mohegan raise his club further for the deathblow. But, his eyes spotted the red, oozing wound in the Mohegan's shoulder. A surge of strength came to Asesakes. He realized, *I have an arrow in my hand!*

Just when the Mohegan's club was raised to its zenith Asesakes jabbed the arrow directly into the Mohegan's wound.

The Mohegan exploded with a howl. He released Asesakes and staggered back several paces. But then, enraged, the Mohegan lunged forward again. The young Manissean fell back onto the trail, *Now I will surely die!*

A blurry shadow caught the corner of Asesakes' eye. The Mohegan was within a few feet from destroying him. A shadowy figure crashed out of the forest and slammed into the side of the Mohegan, driving him into a tree.

Audsah!

The two men fell onto the trail, wrestling. Audsah fought the Mohegan, but even his strength was no match for this demon. The Mohegan soon had Audsah on the ground, holding him with his large hand around the neck. The Mohegan grabbed for the war club with his other hand.

Asesakes took hold of another arrow and jumped up. He sprang onto the Mohegan and drove the arrow into his back. The Mohegan growled and swiped his club around his back, smashing into Asesakes' arm and sending him tumbling back down the trail. He landed with a thud sitting against the base of a tree.

Pain shot to Asesakes' brain as if being seared by a white—hot stone from their hothouse. He glanced down at his lifeless arm. It was shattered. He looked back up to see the Mohegan lifting his arm to bring the club down onto Audsah's head. *This will be Audsah's end—and then mine.*

The Mohegan was bringing his club down, when Asesakes saw something zip out of the forest. Crack! The Mohegan's head jerked. He froze for a moment. The young brave's eyes widened as he watched the Mohegan slowly drop his club. The massive sachem then collapsed onto Audsah.

Asesakes' vision was blurring as he watched Audsah push the Mohegan off him. Then Audsah kicked the Mohegan to confirm that he was unconscious. The sachem did not move. Audsah picked up the Mohegan's war club and dealt the final deathblows, repeatedly bashing his great skull.

Asesakes grimaced and held his shattered arm. The pain radiated throughout his body. The world around him was growing dimmer. *What happened?*

He looked over at Audsah who had his arms raised, waving the club and screeching a loud victory *wôpsukuhq.* *But how?*

Asesakes strained to focus as a figure moved in the forest. He shook his head to clear his vision. His jaw dropped. *Was it the Yôksqáhs?*

Stepping onto the path was the girl, Alsoomse. She searched the ground and found the stone. She picked it up and held it out toward him. It was stained red.

The young brave strained to focus on the girls face as she lifted her head up and stretched her arms high. The moonlight sparkled from her mouth. *Is she smiling?* He looked closer. *No.* She was bearing her teeth like the Island *Natiak.*

Alsoomse then leaned in toward him and shook the stone in his face triumphantly declaring, *"Ni nôhtuy ki!"*

Asesakes nodded and groaned, "Yes, you have shown me." His words trailed off to a whisper. "You are strong."

He felt himself falling. His world went black.

Chapter 10

The Manisseans

The smoke was taken by the island wind and spun into a large funnel. It twirled and hovered over the fire until the wind snapped in the opposite direction, obliterating the vision. Asesakes watched from a distance.

He walked up to the smoldering campfire near the edge of the tall bluff to the east. The old sachem sat quietly, being entertained by the dance between the smoke and the island wind.

They did not speak. The young brave's shattered arm, swollen in shades of black, blue, yellow, and green, was tied to his body to set the breaks. Jacquantu turned away from the dance and looked over at the Mohegans' earthen fort on the center bluff.

Asesakes was about to speak when a weak voice calling for water came from the center bluff. "*Nupi!*" He cringed at the haunting cry and by his own jabbing pain. The pain spiked into his shoulder while he maneuvered to sit down across the fire from Jacquantu.

"Sachem, why do we let this go on? For over a week they have been starved without food and water." He waved his hand in front of his nose. "They smell of rotting flesh.

They cannot fight back. Others desire that we go in and finish them."

"I know that is what others want." The sachem said. "We can now make war is what some say. People who make war, we are not. We are people of Manisses." He scooped up some soft dirt and sand and let it sift through his fingers. "It is what Manisses gives and takes that brought revenge on those Mohegans. The Mohegan and the Pequot people will never be afraid of us, but they will fear Manisses. But my spirit"—he searched for the right word—"it is *sawáyu*—empty. Have we acted as people we were not created to be? Is there a way better for us?"

"My spirit is also *sawáyu.*" Asesakes nodded. "We are not fighters is my belief. But, when we killed the Mohegan sachem something strange happened."

The old man poked at the fire. "What about that was strange?"

"Audsah wanted to kill me and the girl, Alsoomse you know?"

"Yes, I heard." He shook his head. "But I do not think he would."

"Well, a spirit came upon me to say that my life stood between the Mohegan Sachem and Audsah—one was going to kill me. I had no hope, so I cried up to the sky for someone—anyone to save me. Then this fight between the Mohegan Sachem and Audsah happened." He tried to raise his arm as he spoke and groaned. "Well, it happened that Audsah saved me from the Mohegan, and then me and Alsoomse saved Audsah from the Mohegan."

73

"Yes." The sachem kept his eyes on the twisting smoke. "What does that mean to you?"

"The Mohegan is now dead and Audsah's honor is restored. I am now safe." He picked up a small stone and threw it into the fire. "How does such a thing happen?"

Jacquantu continued to watch the smoke and wind dance as he pondered. "Did you not cry out to the sky?"

"I did."

"Then, perhaps it was Manisses' little god?" His eyes widened and he thrust his index finger into the air. "There also is a bigger God. A *wuyi Manto*—a good God." He looked up to the sky. "When this God will step into our lives we never know." He grinned and pointed at Asesakes with his walking stick. "With this spirit, you must have great favor. Perhaps we should call out to this God more often?" With certainty he nodded, "Yes, we should."

Asesakes meditated on the sachem's words. "Still, I fear that spirit of these Mohegans will come back one day to avenge any evil we have done. The Mohegan sachem said he would."

Jacquantu's bushy eyebrows raised up and he peered at Asesakes. "He said that?"

"Yes. Destroy us all one day, he said."

The sachem paused and then reached over to pull a flower from the nearby bush. "A *maci uyuqôm* I had while sleeping last night. You have made me remember." He studied the flower. "In my bad dream, Mohegan Quttajuia came back, and like eating the pink flowers of this beach rose, he began to devour us."

Asesakes' stomach tightened. "Can we stop that from happening?"

Jacquantu crushed the flower in his fingers. "Maybe, but a peace sacrifice there must be." He opened his hand and the wind blew the crushed flower petals away. "With no peace sacrifice, revenge can never die for people in this life. The past won't let it. If people forget, peace spirits will remind them."

"What will have to be sacrificed to save us?"

"Maybe it is one of us? Maybe it is the great sachem of our brother Narragansets? Maybe it is Manisses Island itself? I do not know." He sighed. "We will see."

The young brave felt a sadness sweep over him. "How will we ever know?"

"Let us go *pisupá* in our sweat-lodge." Jacquantu struggled to stand. "It will bring healing to my feet and to your arm." He pointed to his ear. "It is there I often hear from the little god. The old man straightened up. "Perhaps the one who saved you will tell us."

Movement on the center bluff drew Asesakes' attention. He watched as the weakened body of one of the Mohegans crawled out of their earthen fort toward the edge of the bluff. Asesakes pointed. "Jacquantu, another of Mohegans is there. Is that the last one?"

They watched the Mohegan raise himself up and then stumble until he fell off the edge. Asesakes listened. Quiet. No scream. No sound.

"Will Mohegans one day destroy us?" Jacquantu rubbed his chin. "Perhaps." He nodded toward the center bluff. "For now, on this island that is the last of them."

"Well," The old sachem corrected himself, "there is one who fell that may be alive, but he is broken, still hanging onto a rock and moaning this morning." He waved his hand. "You take some men over and look to see if any are still alive. If they are alive, then leave them to Manisses."

Jacquantu limped away.

Asesakes called to him, "But, if they are dead?"

The sachem stopped. He shrugged. "Throw the bodies off the bluff and leave them to Manisses."

Next in the Block Island Settlement Series —
The Fate of Captain John Oldham

Appendix I – Imagined Map of 1633 Block Island

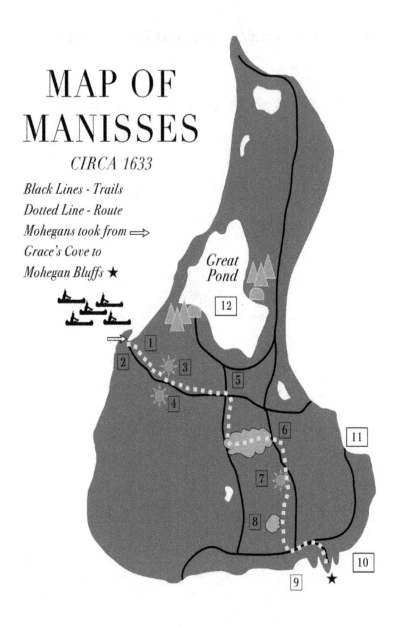

MAP OF MANISSES

CIRCA 1633

Black Lines - Trails
Dotted Line - Route
Mohegans took from ⟹
Grace's Cove to
Mohegan Bluffs ★

Great
Pond

Event Locations

1. Crooked Finger Cove (Grace's Cove)
2. Gravel Hill (Sandy Hill)
3. Between Two Hills (Beacon Hill)
4. Mouwneit Hill
5. Cove Trail crosses Center Trail (Mohegans Attacked by Block Island Dogs)
6. The Great Swamp
7. High ground where Mohegans camped (Pilot Hill)
8. Island Peat Bog (John E's Pond)
9. Shwi Wôkáyu Niputash – Three Jagged Teeth. The tallest of the Southeast Bluffs (Mohegans driven to the Center Bluff)
10. The Mohegan Earthen Fort located on Center Bluff
11. Stoney Beach (Gathering of Seaweed)
12. East and West Great Pond Manissean Villages and Hothouses

Route Manisseans took to drive Mohegans off the bluffs

- Manissean war party leaves the island but spots the Mohegan war party and returns to Manisses
- 50 Mohegans arrive at midnight in 5 long wooden canoes from Stonington to Graces Cove and move east along the narrow trails thru the dunes.
- The Mohegans hike through the woods between the two high hills of Beacon Hill and Mouwneit Hill.
- The Mohegans arrive at the Center trail and head north but run into the island dogs. The dogs are unleashed to chase them south.
- The whole Island tribe lines along the path armed to drive Mohegans southeast towards the tallest bluffs.
- The Mohegans cross the Great Swamp but get bogged down and the entire island tribe gathers to encircle them leaving only one route to the southeast to try to escape.
- Once out of the Swamp they are driven further south along the High Trail.
- They stop at the high point of Pilot Hill to rest but then continue south hoping to reach the beach and escape back to their boats.

- The Mohegans stop at John E's Pond for water and are again attacked by dogs. Several Mohegan Braves fall into a deep tug hole and drown.

- The Mohegans continue south on the trail until they reach the southeast trail where a large contingent of island warriors meets them.

- The Manisseans drive them off the trail to a small trail that runs through the heavy forest and out to the tallest bluff.

- The Mohegans run to the very edge of the bluff and see that there is no escape down.

- The Mohegans are now surrounded with no escape in an open area with forest filled with armed Manisseans in front of them and the steep 200—foot bluff behind them. Arrows rain down on them. They are exposed so the use their hatchets and their axes to dig and build up mounds of dirt for protection.

- Day and night the Island Indians stand watch in the forest and down below on the beach. They continuously rain arrows on the Mohegans.

- The Mohegans are trapped and slowly starved of food and water.

Appendix II – Historical References

1. The Manissean Sachems
2. Audsah
3. The Gravel Hill (Sandy Hill)
4. A Mohegan Raiding Party from Montauk or Quinnehtukqut.
5. West Beach (Grace's Cove) Location of the landing of the Mohegan war party
6. Manisseans destroy Mohegan canoes.
7. Location of Manissean Indian Villages
8. The Dogs of Block Island
9. The Island Swamp
10. The Island Peat Bogs
11. The Bluffs
12. Island Seaweed
13. The Mohegan Earthworks
14. Description of Manissean deaths
15. Hothouses

1. **Block Island Sachems**

    HISTORY OF BLOCK ISLAND by Rev. S. T.
    LIVERMORE

    Page 288 – "To Mr. Edward Ball, and the rest of the
    town council: Whereof, **Penewess** the late sachem being
    dead to whom the land reserved for him belonged, and
    now belongeth to his countrymen whereof Ninicraft
    being willing for to assist them in the putting of the land
    to rent so as for to be at a certainty of receiving rent
    yearly for it, I pray you let there be no bar nor hindrance
    towards that proceeding, but rather be helpful to them in
    the matter, for it is fit that they should make the best
    improvement they can of what belongs to them; which is
    all 1 have to trouble you with at present, remaining
    yours to serve in any thing that I am capable.   Simon
    Ray, "Warden."

    WINTHROP'S HISTORY OF NEW ENGLAND by
    John Winthrop
    Page 218 –From **Jacquantu**, Block Island Sachem, that
    he is preparing 13 fathom of white and 2 of blue to
    present you with about the 1st Month. (1637)

2. Audsah

HISTORY OF BLOCK ISLAND by Rev. S. T. LIVERMORE

Page 14 — In a letter from Roger Williams to Gov. Winthrop in 1637, the former stated that the sachems of the Narragansetts had left the Block Island Indians to the governor, at the time of Mr. Oldham's death, and "so have done since " that said sachems had sought the head of; *Audsah,* the murderer of Oldham.

Page 57 — We can easily imagine their lordly bearing, as several of these chiefs looked upon the vessel of Oldham anchored upon their shores, and as they laid the plot to seize his goods and take his life. The ringleader's name was Audsah, and he struck the fatal blows—fatal not only to Mr. Oldham, but also to the Indian life on Block Island. The fatal seed he then planted yielded him and his fellow Islanders a fearful harvest. Audsah, like Cain, became a fugitive, was hunted from tribe to tribe, and at one time was sheltered on the main by one Wequashcuck, a petty sachem.

3. **Gravel Hill (Sandy Hill)**

HISTORY OF BLOCK ISLAND by Rev. S. T. LIVERMORE

Page 164 — Sandy Hill, there, arrests the attention of the visitor. It is near the Sound shore, with a base a quarter of a mile long from' north to south, and half that distance east and west, rising about one hundred feet to a point on which half a dozen horses might stand, affording a fine view of the sea, of Montauk, and of Watch Hill, and also of the west shore of the Island. It is a pile of drift, and would be worth a fortune for sand and gravel if properly located. It is almost wholly destitute of vegetation, except the tuft of grass on the top which makes the tout—ensemble look somewhat like a Chinese head. Its base rests upon a bed of peat, which shows that it was thrown up after the Island had produced vegetation. At its eastern foot is a famous deposit of "firing," "tug," or peat, as it is called.

4. **A Mohegan Raiding Party from Montauk or Quinnehtukqut.**

HISTORY OF BLOCK ISLAND by Rev. S. T. LIVERMORE

Page 58 — "The Indians on this Island had war with the Mohegan Indians, although the Island lies in the ocean and open seas, four leagues from the nearest mainland, and much farther distant from any Island, and from the nearest place of landing to the Mohegan country forty miles, I suppose at least, through a hideous wilderness, as it then was, besides the difficulty of two large rivers. To prosecute their designed hostilities each party furnished themselves with a large fleet of canoes, furnished with bows and arrows.

Page 50 — Island then, three hundred and fifty years ago, when the aboriginal lords of the soil, never disturbed by the face of a white man, with their squaws and papooses, sat around their summer evening fires, eating their succotash, hominy, clams, fish, and wild game, braiding mats and baskets, and repeating the traditions of their forefathers, or in their wild war dances, with painted faces, with demon yells and grimaces and horrid threats, celebrating their victories over invaders from the Mohegans of Montauk, or the Pequots from the mainland.

5. **West Beach (Grace's Cove)**
HISTORY OF BLOCK ISLAND by Rev. S. T. LIVERMORE
Page 164 – Grace's Cove is near Sandy Hill, and the place it occupies is sometimes call Grace's Point, and has been distinguished somewhat as a place for landing small boats. It was there, probably, that the Mohegan Indians landed when they came by moonlight from Stonington, or Watch Hill, in force, to fight the Manisseans, and were so barbarously destroyed at Mohegan Bluff.

Page 69 — Still, it was within reach of the eagle—eyed Sassacus and his warlike Pequots, and even the more distant Mohegans beyond the Connecticut river coveted the fertile plantations and productive fishing grounds of Manisses. Tradition points to their savage fleet of bark canoes launched beyond "two large rivers," and made to skim over the briny deep by the force of paddles flashing in the moonlight until they were silently dipped at midnight along the Island's shores at Cooneymus, or at Grace's Cove. It tells us too of the Mohegan dashes from Montauk, their shortest distance to row to Manisses.

6. Manisseans destroy Mohegan canoes.

HISTORY OF BLOCK ISLAND by Rev. S. T. LIVERMORE

Page 56 — "Both being on the seas, it being in the night arid moonshine, and by the advantage of it the Block Islanders discovered the Mohegans, but they saw not the Islanders. Upon which these turned back to their own shore, and hauled their canoes out of sight, and waylaid their enemies until they landed, and marched up in the Island, and then stove all their [the Mohegans'] canoes,

7. Location of Manissean Indian Villages

HISTORY OF BLOCK ISLAND by Rev. S. T. LIVERMORE

Page 57 — The shores of the Great Pond were evidently the most thickly settled by the Indians. About it Roger Williams discovered the wigwams of several petty sachems. Thither they resorted for fish, clams, oysters, and scallops, as large deposits of shells now occasionally opened testify.

8. The Dogs of Block Island

HISTORY OF BLOCK ISLAND by Rev. S. T. LIVERMORE

Page 58 — The " dogs " of Block Island belonging to the Manisseans before the English came have their descendants here still, it is believed. They are not numerous, but peculiar, differing materially from all the species which we have noticed on the main—land, both in figure and dis— position. They are below a medium size, with short legs but powerful, broad breasts, heavy quarters, massive head unlike the bull dog, the terrier, the hound, the mastiff, but resembling mostly the last; with a fierce disposition that in some makes but little distinction between friend and foe. In Jan., 1719, by an act of the town, the Indians were not allowed to keep dogs.

In 1860, a visitor on the Island wrote: "There are not one—fourth as many sheep here as there ought to be, and as there would be, if it were not for that crying nuisance, the multiplicity of dogs. The farmers dare not risk the dangers from canine depredations which, at the present time, are full as great as when wolves howled over the ancient hills of the Island." Query: Did the Island ever have wolves? The dogs then were very numerous, and wanted a change from fish diet. They also killed geese, a large flock in one instance, and buried them, as a future supply of fresh meat. The dogs now are more civilized, perhaps better fed.

9. The Island's Great Swamp

HISTORY OF BLOCK ISLAND by Rev. S. T. LIVERMORE

Page 54 — "The next day we set upon our march, the Indians being retired into swamps, so as we could not find them. We burnt and spoiled both houses and corn in great abundance, but they kept themselves in obscurity. Captain Turner stepping aside to a swamp met with some few Indians, and charged upon them, changing some few bullets for arrows.

That Captain James Sands had a stone house, used as a garrison and hospital, in times of necessity, is admitted, and shown by Mr. Niles' History. . . Mr. Niles, when the French landed, was " in fair sight of the house," and at the same time "saw them coming from the water—side," while just behind him was a " large swamp.""

Page 286 — The "upland in a great swamp" to which Mr. Niles fled the first time the French came to Mr. Sands' house, was a convenient place of concealment, lying a short distance northwest of the location of said house. The upland and swamp remain, and are easily pointed out, lying a little distance west of Erastus Rose's house.

10. The Island Peat Bogs

HISTORY OF BLOCK ISLAND by Rev. S. T. LIVERMORE

Page 22 — The settlers found perhaps a better soil than they left in Massachusetts. The inexhaustible stores of peat in the little swamps of the Island are evidence of the fertility of the soil which produced those stores composed of leaves, bark, nuts, roots, and decayed wood, all of which were washed down the little steep hills into the little deep valleys at their feet.

Page 28 — The beds are also numerous, and in every part of the Island. Some cover several acres, and others are much smaller. Some are shallow, and others are deep, and most of them were formed by vegetable matter, leaves, bark, nuts, grass, ferns, decayed wood, etc., that for ages had been washed down the surrounding steep hillsides. Thus peat beds were deposited upon some of the highest parts of the Island, as upon Clay Head, and the supply was ample, if not exhaustless.

The present quantity of peat on the Island cannot be estimated easily. Those best prepared to judge readily, admit that if the present population, eleven hundred and fifty, were to remain uniform for a hundred years, with no other fuel than the peat which they now have, their supply would be abundant. Three beds of considerable known size, that may be very much larger than known to be, one on the east side of the Island, and two on the west, extend a considerable distance from the shore into the ocean.

Page 174 — Is there a portion of the Island sinking? Has a cavern been forming there by the escape of clay or quicksand? A larger portion of Mohegan Bluff has settled similarly. Has there been a crushing of coral beneath the Island? Native coral has

11. The Bluffs (Mohegan Bluffs)

HISTORY OF BLOCK ISLAND by Rev. S. T. LIVERMORE

Pages 167—168 — Mohegan Bluffs proper, belongs to the West Side according to tradition. It is the high point next to the sea where the Mohegan warriors were penned up and starved by the Manisseans. The former in coming to the Island would naturally land on the West Side, at Grace's Cove, Dorry's Cove, or Cooneymus, as the "Moheague country " was lying to the northwest of the Island. Soon after they landed, Niles says, the Manisseans "drove them to the opposite part of the Island, where, I suppose, the cliffs next the sea are near, if not more than two hundred feet high." This account

seems to locate Mohegan Bluff near the new light—
house. But as a compromise the name may well apply to
the entire bluff range across the south end of the Island.
"Bluff" is more appropriate than " Cliff," as there are no
rocks.

12. Island Seaweed

HISTORY OF BLOCK ISLAND by Rev. S. T.
LIVERMORE

Page 30 — Without the grasses torn from the rocks
along the shore, and from the meadows on the bottom of
the sea—torn loose and driven upon the shores during
the storms of autumn, winter, and spring, the farms of
Block Island, long ago, would have become utterly
barren.

Page 31—32 — The quantity of sea—weed used upon
the Island is immense. The annual gathering begins in
October and continues, at intervals, until April. The
portions of the beach owned by the town exhibit the
greatest industry. There the weed is common property,
and those who are there first in the morning, latest at

night, and wade into the surf the deepest, are generally most profited, excepting those who thus secure a crop of pains called rheumatic.

This kind of industry, common and private, on public and individual beaches, secures an annual value that could not be bought of the Islanders for twenty thousand dollars, nor could they get an equal quantity of fertilizers from abroad for fifty thousand dollars. Its quantity, as reported by the last census, was six thousand cords, gathered on the shores of Block Island in the year 1875. This quantity is equal to over ten thousand single team loads, and each load is worth more than two dollars. Hence, this resource of the Island, during the period of twenty—five years, amounts to the handsome sum, or its equivalent, of half a million of dollars.

That sea—weed is an indispensable resource here is demonstrated thus: Without it the Island would become sterile; without a productive soil, here the population could not be supported, since for that the fisheries are inadequate, and neither manufacturing nor commerce here exists. But the Islander rejoices in the abundance of the sea which supplies him with fish as well as with vegetation.

13. The Mohegan Earthworks/Fort/Trench

HISTORY OF BLOCK ISLAND by Rev. S. T. LIVERMORE

Page 56 — The Mohegans dug in at the edge of the bluff and the islanders kept them confined without food or water.

Page 57 — They had indeed by some means dug a trench around them toward the land to defend them from the arrows of their enemies, which I have seen, and it is called the Mohegan Fort to this day."
That fort, probably, has long since sloughed off into the sea by the action of frosts and rains upon the bluffs for more than a century. All personal knowledge of it has also faded away from the Islanders.

14. Description of Manissean deaths

HISTORY OF BLOCK ISLAND by Rev. S. T. LIVERMORE

Page 67 — Buried eatables with the dead in a jar to supply them with food on their journey to another world. Buried standing in a walking posture.

Believed in the existence of the power of a great spirit, a belief in a conscious future state and a soul's immortality.

Page 68 — The old Indian burial ground at Indian head neck.

15. Hothouse

HISTORY OF BLOCK ISLAND by Rev. S. T. LIVERMORE

Page 59 — Hot houses were made partly underground, and in the form of a large oven, where two or three persons might on occasion sit together, and it was place near some depth of water. Their method was to heat some stones very hot in the fire, and put them into the hot house, and when the person(s) were in, to shut it close up, with only so much air as was necessary for respiration or that they within might freely draw their breath. They would sweat in a prodigious manner, stay in the sweat house as long as they could possibly stand it and then rush out to plunge into the nearby water. This was their cure for all types of pains and numbness of joints and many maladies. Located in the bank near the water on the south end of the great pond towards the west.

Appendix III – Historical Resources

- The History of Block Island – S.T. Livermore
- The History of the state of Rhode Island and Providence Plantations — Reverend Samuel Niles
- Relation of the Pequot Warres (1660) — Lion Gardener
- Historical Sketch of Block Island – William P. Sheffield
- Winthrop's History of New England – John Winthrop
- The History of the State if Rhode Island
- A Modern Mohegan Dictionary 2006 Edition by Stephanie Fielding
- History of Long Island from Its Discovery and Settlement — Benjamin Franklin Thompson

1661 Block Island Map (Cover art) published with permission by the Rhode Island Historical Society

Appendix IV – Algonquin Words

Chapter 1

- Asesakes – Eyes of an eagle
- Wáwôtam – Careful, Cunning, Wise
- Inak – Man/Men
- Mucuhcôqak kisqutu – Spirit Angry
- Mikucut – Dung
- Mutu – No
- Quinnehtukqut — Connecticut
- Ahqi – Stop
- Wôpsukuhq — Eagle cry
- Alsoomse – Independent
- Yôksqáhs – Older girl
- Kôkci citsak – Fat bird
- Kipi — Quickly
- Nicish — Hands
- Nuks — Yes
- Yakus pakitam – Stomach throw
- Muhshoyash — Canoes

Chapter 2

- Wôkáyu icuk — Crooked Finger
- Muhshaki nupsapáq — Great Pond
- Asoku - Foolish
- Patáhqáham – Thunder
- Wôwôsôpshá — Lightening
- Kisi – Finished

- Kuhthan wunipaqash – Sea leaves

Chapter 3
- Mingan — Gray wolf
- Mosopish — Shells
- Suksuwak – long clams
- Wiwáhcumunsh — Corn
- Wáci – purpose
- Citsak — Baby birds
- Muksak — wolves
- Wikôtamuwôk – Fun
- Sqahsihsak – little girls
- Wisôsu — Frightened
- Natiak — Dogs
- Nuskinoqat natiak – Dirty, unclean dogs
- Uyutáháwôk – Emotion, Feeling
- Páhpohs – Baby

Chapter 4
- Ahqi – Hurry
- Mahcáq - Swamp
- Sihsiqak – Snakes
- Akômuk — across water
- Pumôtam — Alive
- Awán na skitôpak – Who are you people?

Chapter 5
- Ayumohs – Puppy

- Woonanit — Good spirit
- Mattanit — Bad spirit

Chapter 6
- Kôkci ohqák – Maggots
- Wisôsu — Afraid
- Páhpohs – Baby

Chapter 7
- Kuhthan – Ocean
- Kuhthan wunipaqash – Sea leaves

Chapter 8
- Mômôci – Move
- Cáyhqatum – Be in a hurry
- Wihpqat – Tastes good
- Uyutáhá — Feel a certain way

Chapter 9
- Iyo – Go
- Yôkôpák — Older boys
- Wisôsu kôcuci ohq mikucut – Scared little worm dung
- Ni nôhtuy ki – I show you

Chapter 10
- Nupi – Water
- Sawáyu – Empty

- **maci uyuqôm – Wicked/Bad/Evil Dream**
- **Wuyi manto – A Good God**
- **Pisupá — Sweat**

Next in the Block Island Settlement Series —
  The Fate of Captain John Oldham

Cover Map:
Courtesy the Rhode Island Historical Society. Item RHi 4682. A Chart of Block Island Agreeable to a Survey made by the direction and for the benefit of the Original Proprietors. Block Island, RI. 1661. Graphics Map #1400 Copyright Rhode Island Historical Society

David Lee Tucker contact info:
Email: Dleetucker@gmail.com
Blog: tuckedin-lampsburning.com

Made in the USA
Middletown, DE
22 August 2023

37169206R00189